Well done Zain!
The first paragraph of your homework had me gripped and it was enough to convince me
that we together as a family can develop this story and produce a book.
Thanks to Ami and Mummy as well who were full of vision and inspiring ideas!

MUHAMMAD ALIM

This book is published by
Grosvenor House Publishing Ltd
Link House
140 The Broadway, Tolworth, Surrey, KT6 7HT.
www.grosvenorhousepublishing.co.uk

A CIP record for this book
is available from the British Library

Paperback ISBN 978-1-80381-408-7
Hardback ISBN 978-1-80381-407-0
eBook ISBN 978-1-80381-409-4

ZAIN'S SPACE ADVENTURE

Written by Muhammad Alim

Illustrated by Shi LianXin

Grosvenor House
Publishing Limited

Zain wakes up and realises it is eerily silent.

He waits one more second but
still can't hear anything.

"Where am I?"

"How did I get here?"

Zain mutters to himself.

4

Zain looks around the room but it's empty.

He notices a door in the distance.

So he quickly moves towards it and
then rushes outside.

Zain is shocked.

He can see planet Earth on the horizon.

Zain runs towards planet Earth,
but space is endless and
doesn't make much progress.

He looks around and can see planets
all around him.

Zain runs towards the nearest planet and notices a door.

He opens the door and rushes inside.

Zain is amazed.

He is on planet **Mercury.**

Zain realises Mercury is the smallest planet in our solar system and the closest to the sun.

Mercury is not the hottest planet because it has almost no atmosphere to trap the heat.

Zain then notices another door in the distance.

He runs towards it.

Opens the door and rushes inside.

Zain is agitated.

He is on planet **Venus.**

Zain realises Venus is the hottest planet and
spins in the opposite direction to
Earth and most other planets.

One day on Venus is the same as 243 days on Earth.

Zain notices another door in the distance.

He runs towards it.

Opens the door and rushes inside.

Zain is jubilant.

He is on planet **Earth.**

Zain realises Earth is our home and is the only planet that has living creatures on it.

Earth's surface consists mainly of water.

Zain notices another door in the distance.

He runs towards it.

Opens the door and rushes inside.

Zain is captivated.

He is on planet **Mars.**

Zain realises Mars is very cold and dry.

It has many craters, deep valleys, and volcanoes.

Zain then notices another door in the distance.

He runs towards it.

Opens the door and rushes inside.

Zain is terrified.

He is on planet **Jupiter.**

Zain realises Jupiter is the largest planet.

It has a 'Great Red Spot' which is a storm that has been blowing for hundreds of years.

Zain notices another door in the distance.

He runs towards it.

Opens the door and rushes inside.

Zain is mystified.

He is on planet **Saturn.**

Zain realises Saturn is the second largest
planet and famous for its rings.

The rings are made of chunks of ice and rock.

Zain notices another door in the distance.

He runs towards it.

Opens the door and rushes inside.

Zain is despondent.

He is on planet **Uranus.**

Zain realises Uranus is the coldest planet and unlike any other planet, rotates on its side.

Clouds on Uranus can circle at over 300mph.

Zain notices another door in the distance.

He runs towards it.

Opens the door and rushes inside.

Zain is exhilarated.

He is on planet **Neptune.**

Zain realises Neptune is cold, dark, and very windy.

Neptune is the last planet in our solar system.

Zain then notices another door in the distance.

He runs towards it.

Opens the door and rushes inside.

44

Zain is bewildered.

He's in a pitch-black room.

"What am I doing here?"
Zain mutters to himself.

Suddenly Zain can hear a sound getting closer.

"Wake up!" his little sister yells.

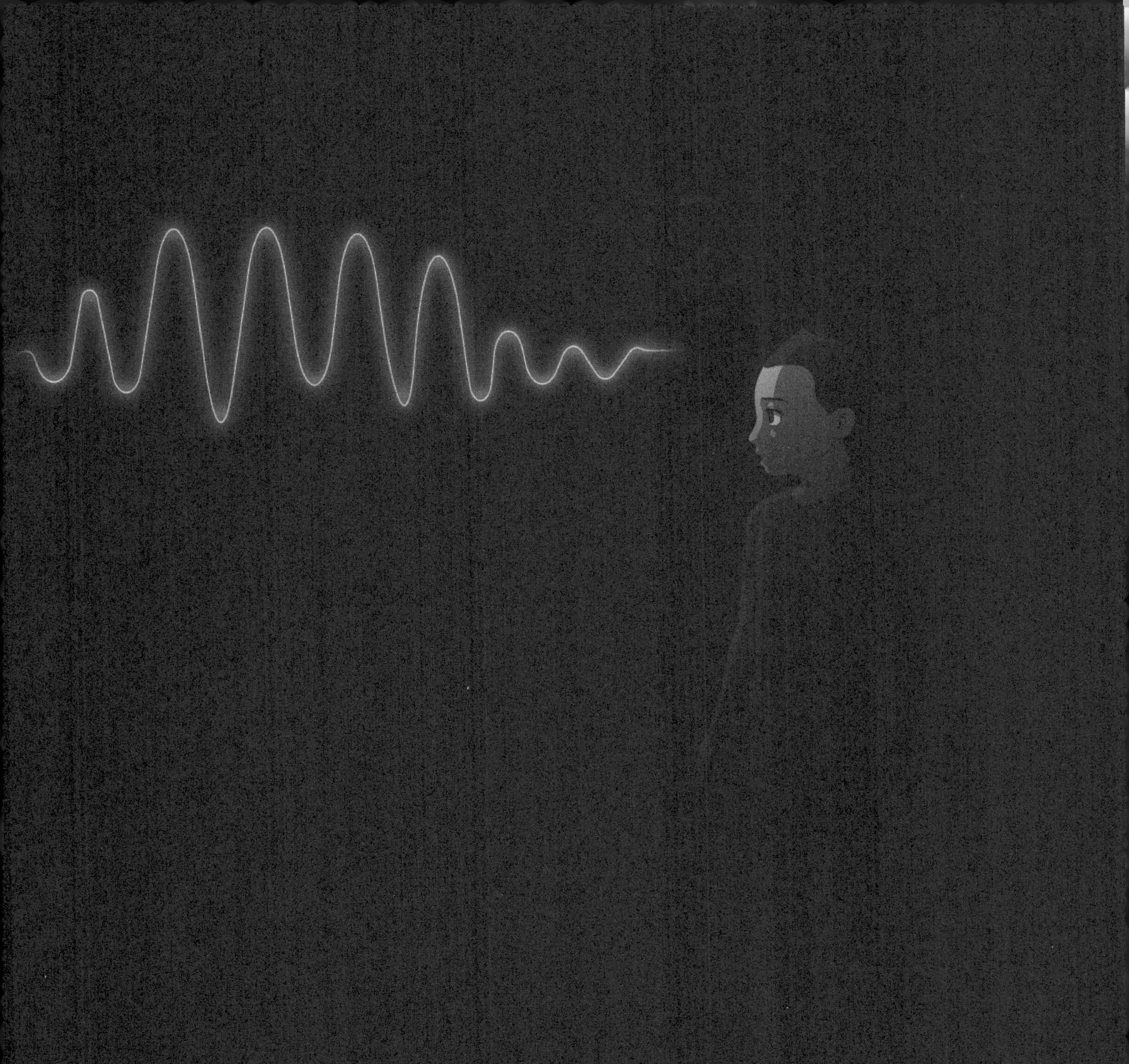

Zain opens his eyes and hears his little sister say, "Get ready! We're going to the space museum."

Zain smiles and realises it was all just a dream.

THE END

Milton Keynes UK
Ingram Content Group UK Ltd.
UKHW052357140823
426856UK00007B/28

9 781803 814087